Lon Po Po

A Red-Riding Hood Story from China

Translated and Illustrated by

Ed Young

PaperStar

Penguin Young Readers Group

To all the wolves of the world
for lending their good name
as a tangible symbol
for our darkness.

Once, long ago, there was a woman who lived alone in the country with her three children, Shang, Tao, and Paotze. On the day of their grandmother's birthday, the good mother set off to see her, leaving the three children at home.

Before she left, she said, "Be good while I am away, my heart-loving children; I will not return tonight. Remember to close the door tight at sunset and latch it well."

But an old wolf lived nearby and saw the good mother leave. At dusk, disguised as an old woman, he came up to the house of the children and knocked on the door twice: bang, bang.

Shang, who was the eldest, said through the latched door, "Who is it?"

"My little jewels," said the wolf, "this is your grandmother, your Po Po."

"Po Po!" Shang said. "Our mother has gone to visit you!"

The wolf acted surprised. "To visit me? I have not met her along the way. She must have taken a different route."

"Po Po!" Shang said. "How is it that you come so late?"

The wolf answered, "The journey is long, my children, and the day is short."

Shang listened through the door. "Po Po," she said, "why is your voice so low?"

"Your grandmother has caught a cold, good children, and it is dark and windy out here. Quickly open up, and let your Po Po come in," the cunning wolf said.

Tao and Paotze could not wait. One unlatched the door and the other opened it. They shouted, "Po Po, Po Po, come in!"

At the moment he entered the door, the wolf blew out the candle.

"Po Po," Shang asked, "why did you blow out the candle? The room is now dark."

The wolf did not answer.

Tao and Paotze rushed to their Po Po and wished to be hugged. The old wolf held Tao. "Good child, you are so plump." He embraced Paotze. "Good child, you have grown to be so sweet."

Soon the old wolf pretended to be sleepy. He yawned. "All the chicks are in the coop," he said. "Po Po is sleepy too." When he climbed into the big bed, Paotze climbed in at one end with the wolf, and Shang and Tao climbed in at the other.

But when Shang stretched, she touched the wolf's tail. "Po Po, Po Po, your foot has a bush on it."

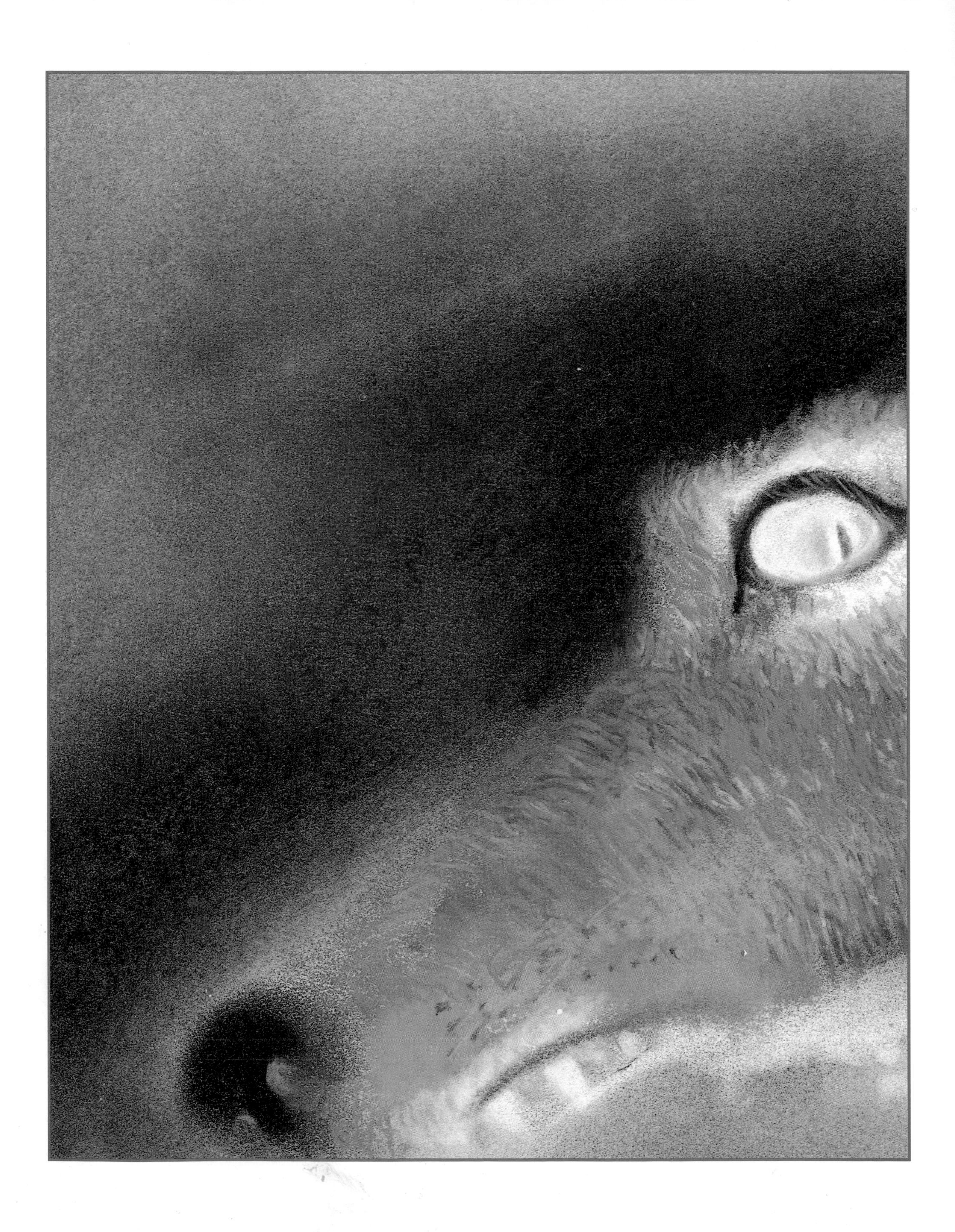

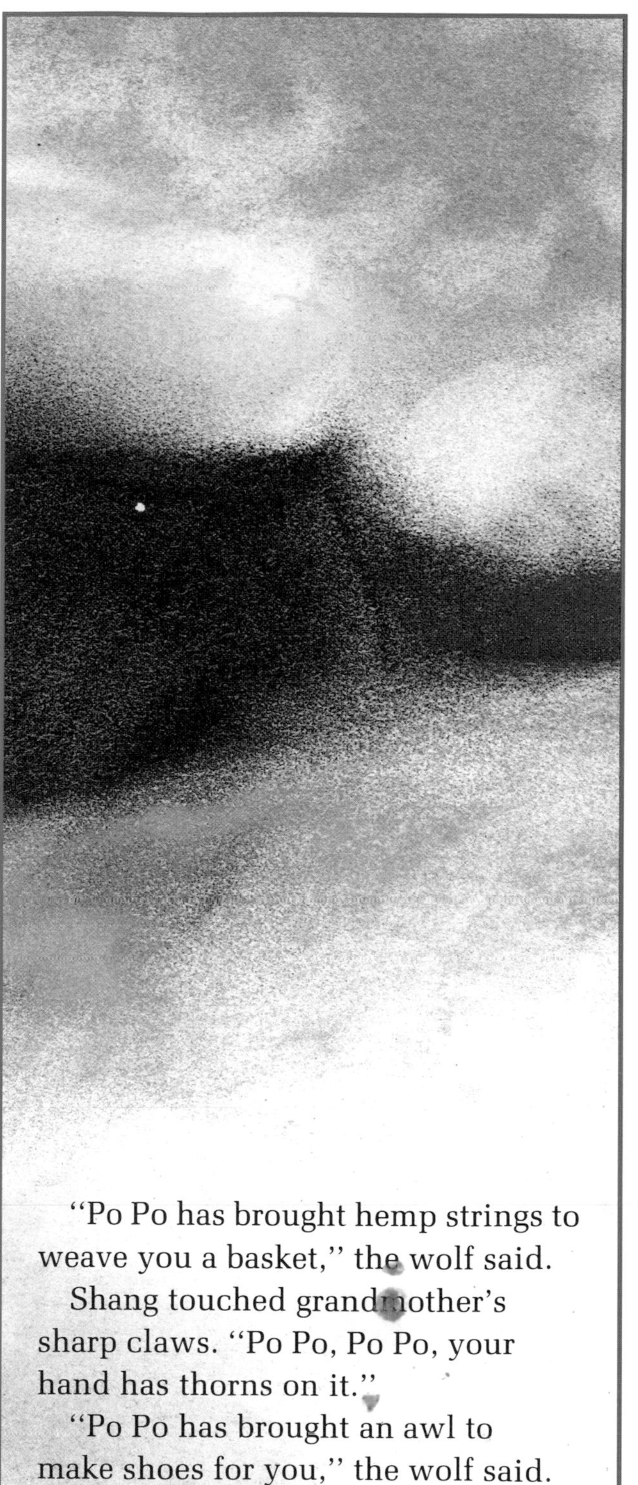

"Po Po has brought hemp strings to weave you a basket," the wolf said.

Shang touched grandmother's sharp claws. "Po Po, Po Po, your hand has thorns on it."

"Po Po has brought an awl to make shoes for you," the wolf said.

At once, Shang lit the light and the wolf blew it out again, but Shang had seen the wolf's hairy face.

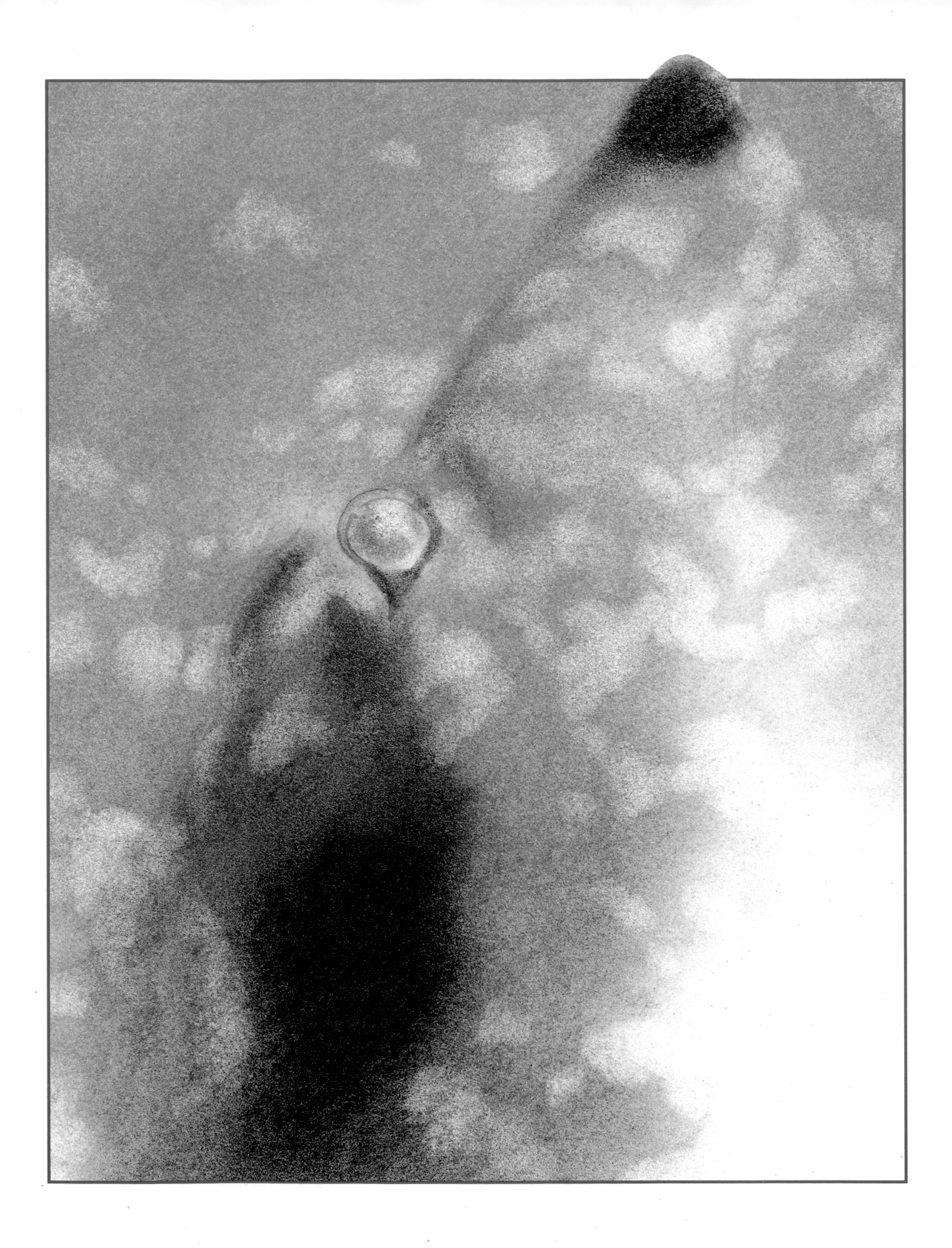

"Po Po, Po Po," she said, for she was not only the eldest, she was the most clever, "you must be hungry. Have you eaten gingko nuts?"

"What is gingko?" the wolf asked.

"Gingko is soft and tender, like the skin of a baby. One taste and you will live forever," Shang said, "and the nuts grow on the top of the tree just outside the door."

The wolf gave a sigh. "Oh, dear. Po Po is old, her bones have become brittle. No longer can she climb trees."

"Good Po Po, we can pick some for you," Shang said.

The wolf was delighted.

Shang jumped out of bed and Tao and Paotze came with her to the gingko tree. There, Shang told her sisters about the wolf and all three climbed up the tall tree.

The wolf waited and waited. Plump Tao did not come back. Sweet Paotze did not come back. Shang did not come back, and no one brought any nuts from the gingko tree. At last the wolf shouted, "Where are you, children?"

"Po Po," Shang called out, "we are on the top of the tree eating gingko nuts."

"Good children," the wolf begged, "pluck some for me."

"But Po Po, gingko is magic only when it is plucked directly from the tree. You must come and pluck it from the tree yourself."

The wolf came outside and paced back and forth under the tree where he heard the three children eating the gingko nuts at the top. "Oh, Po Po, these nuts are so tasty! The skin so tender," Shang said. The wolf's mouth began to water for a taste.

Finally, Shang, the eldest and most clever child, said, "Po Po, Po Po, I have a plan. At the door there is a big basket. Behind it is a rope. Tie the rope to the basket, sit in the basket and throw the other end to me. I can pull you up."

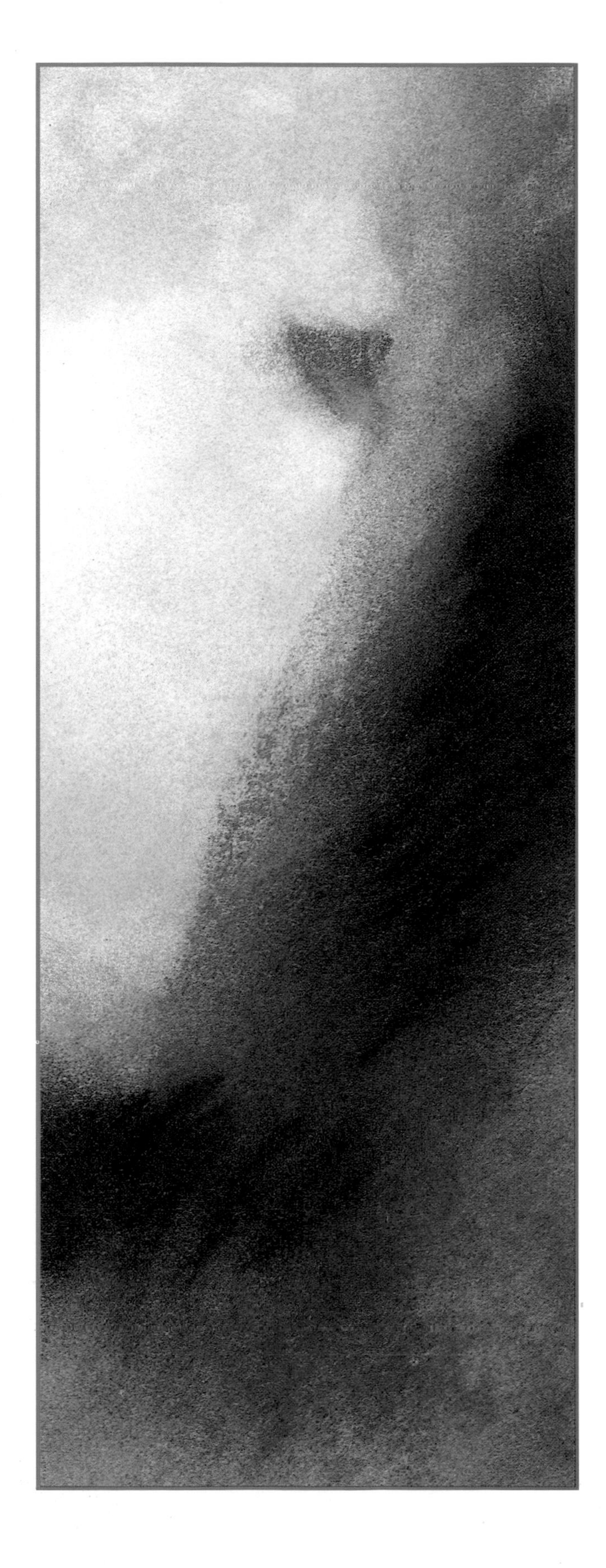

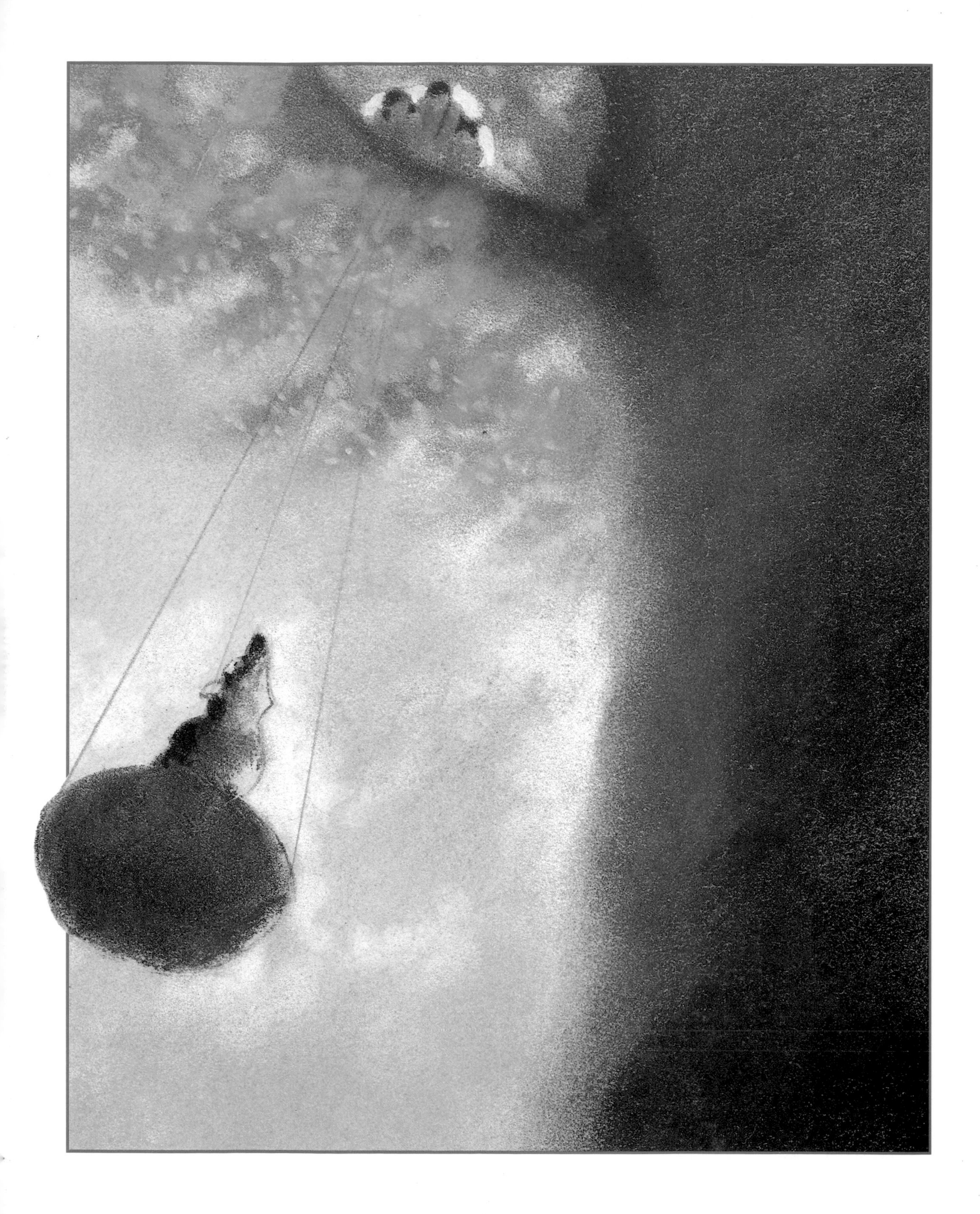

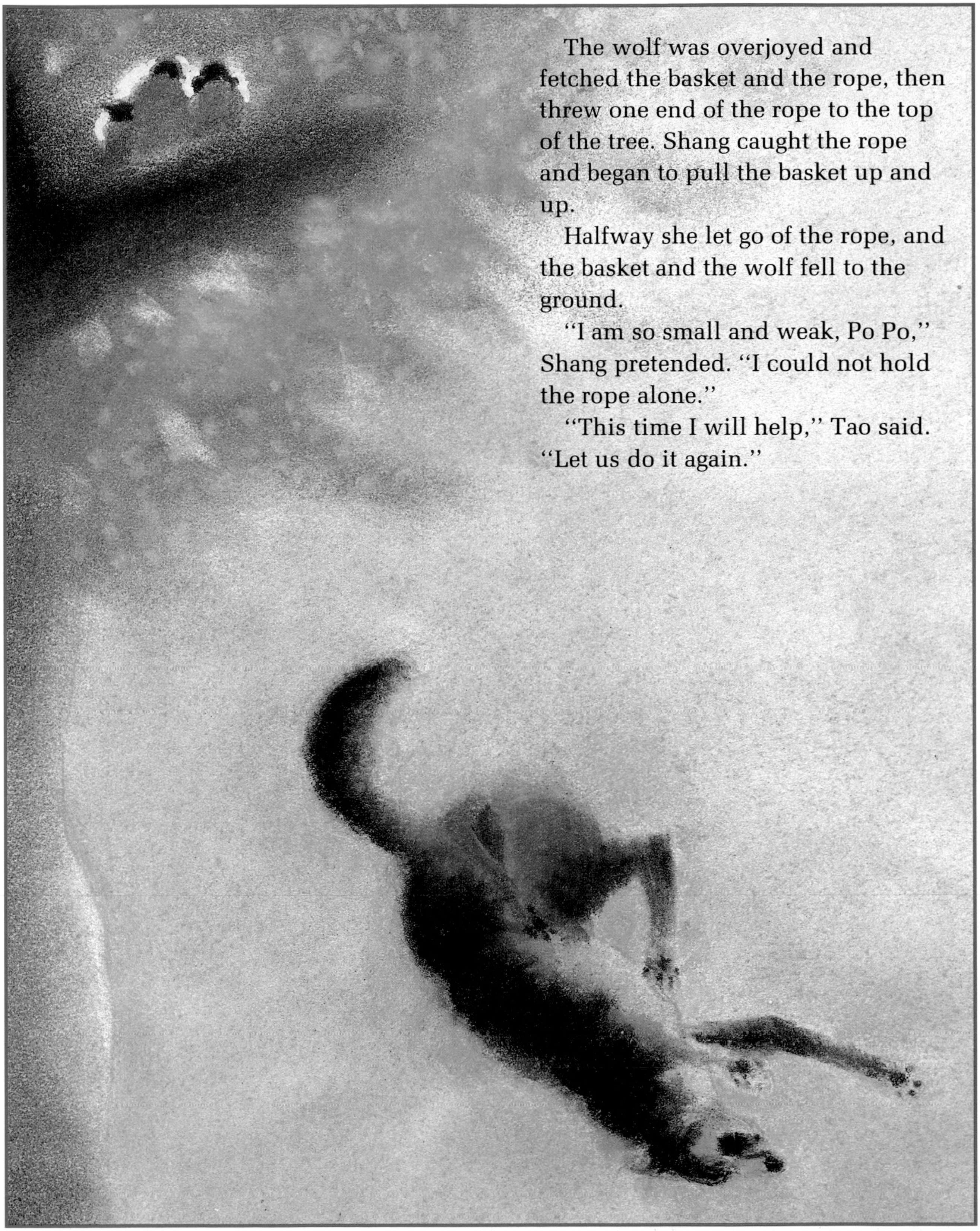

The wolf was overjoyed and fetched the basket and the rope, then threw one end of the rope to the top of the tree. Shang caught the rope and began to pull the basket up and up.

Halfway she let go of the rope, and the basket and the wolf fell to the ground.

"I am so small and weak, Po Po," Shang pretended. "I could not hold the rope alone."

"This time I will help," Tao said. "Let us do it again."

The wolf had only one thought in his mind: to taste a gingko nut. He climbed into the basket again. Now Shang and Tao pulled the rope on the basket together, higher and higher.

Again, they let go, and again the wolf tumbled down, down, and bumped his head.

The wolf was furious. He growled and cursed. "We could not hold the rope, Po Po," Shang said, "but only one gingko nut and you will be well again."

"I shall give a hand to my sisters this time," Paotze, the youngest, said. "This time we shall not fail."

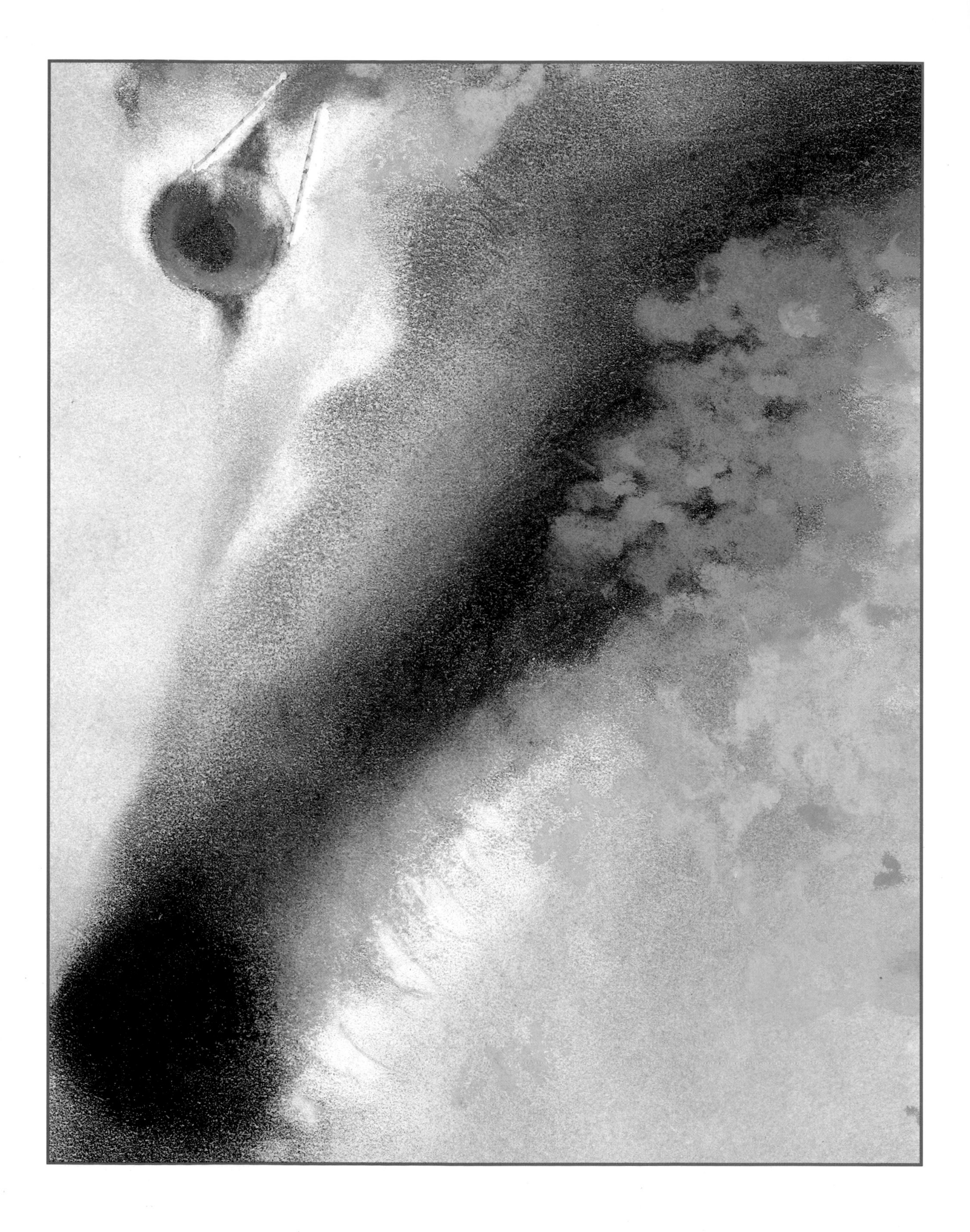

Now the children pulled the rope with all of their strength. As they pulled they sang, "Hei yo, hei yo," and the basket rose straight up, higher than the first time, higher than the second time, higher and higher and higher until it nearly reached the top of the tree. When the wolf reached out, he could almost touch the highest branch.

But at that moment, Shang coughed and they all let go of the rope, and the basket fell down and down and down. Not only did the wolf bump his head, but he broke his heart to pieces.

"Po Po," Shang shouted, but there was no answer.

"Po Po," Tao shouted, but there was no answer.

"Po Po," Paotze shouted. There was still no answer. The children climbed to the branches just above the wolf and saw that he was truly dead. Then they climbed down, went into the house, closed the door, locked the door with the latch and fell peacefully asleep.

On the next day, their mother returned with baskets of food from their real Po Po, and the three sisters told her the story of the Po Po who had come.

A PaperStar Book, published in 1996 by Penguin Putnam Books for Young Readers, 345 Hudson Street, New York, NY 10014.

Originally published in 1989 by Philomel Books, New York.
Published simultaneously in Canada. Manufactured in China
Calligraphy by John Stevens.

Library of Congress Cataloging-in-Publication Data
Young, Ed. Lon Po Po/translated from collection of Chinese folktales and illustrated by Ed Young. p. cm. Summary: Three sisters staying home alone are endangered by a hungry wolf who is disguised as their grandmother. [1. Folklore—China.] I. Title.
PZ8.1.Y84LAN 1989 398.2'0951—dc19 [E] 88-15222 CIP AC
ISBN 978-0-698-11382-4
32 33 34 35 36 37 38 39 40